MARVEL
SPIDER-MAN

THIS IS SPIDER-MAN

Adapted by **Emeli Juhlin**

Illustrated by **Steve Kurth, Mike Huddleston, Geanes Holland, Tomas Montalvos-Lagos, Olga Lepaeva, and Tomasso Moscardini**

Based on the Marvel comic book series **Spider-Man**

MARVEL

Los Angeles
New York

SUSTAINABLE FORESTRY INITIATIVE
Certified Sourcing
www.sfiprogram.org
SFI-01415

Printed in the United States of America
First Edition, September 2021   10 9 8 7 6 5 4 3 2 1
Library of Congress Control Number: 2021930699
FAC-029261-21204
ISBN: 978-1-368-07125-3

This is Peter Parker.

Peter lives in Queens.
Queens is in
New York City.

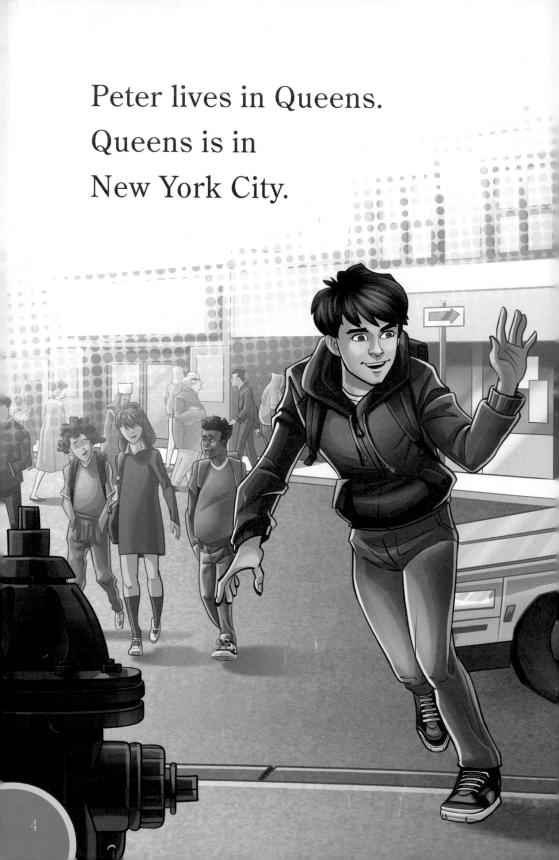

Peter lives with his aunt.

Her name is Aunt May.

Peter loves Aunt May
very much.

Peter is in high school.
He goes to Midtown High.

Peter loves math.

He loves science.

Peter works at the *Daily Bugle*.
He takes pictures.

Peter's boss wants pictures of
Spider-Man.

But Peter has a secret.

Peter *is* Spider-Man!

He was bitten by a spider.

The spider gave him
super-powers!

Spider-Man can climb walls.

He can shoot webs.

Spider-Man has super-strength.

He also has spider-sense.
It warns him of danger.

Venom is in the city!

Venom is no match
for Spider-Man.

Spider-Man fights
a lot of villains.

Not even the Looter
can get away!